FOR MY FAMILY

X X X

First published 2017 by Two Hoots
This edition published 2018 by Two Hoots
an imprint of Pan Macmillan
20 New Wharf Road, London N1 9RR
Associated companies throughout the world
www.panmacmillan.com
ISBN 978-1-5098-5097-6
Text and illustrations copyright © Morag Hood 2017
Moral rights asserted.

1 3 5 7 9 8 6 4 2

A CIP catalogue record for this book is available from the British Library.
Printed in China
The illustrations in this book were created using ink and lino printing.

www.twohootsbooks.com

This **TW🦉HOOTS** book
belongs to

MORAG HOOD

WHEN GRANDAD WAS A PENGUIN

TW🐦 HOOTS

Last time I went to stay with Grandad, he seemed a little different.

He talked a lot about fishing.

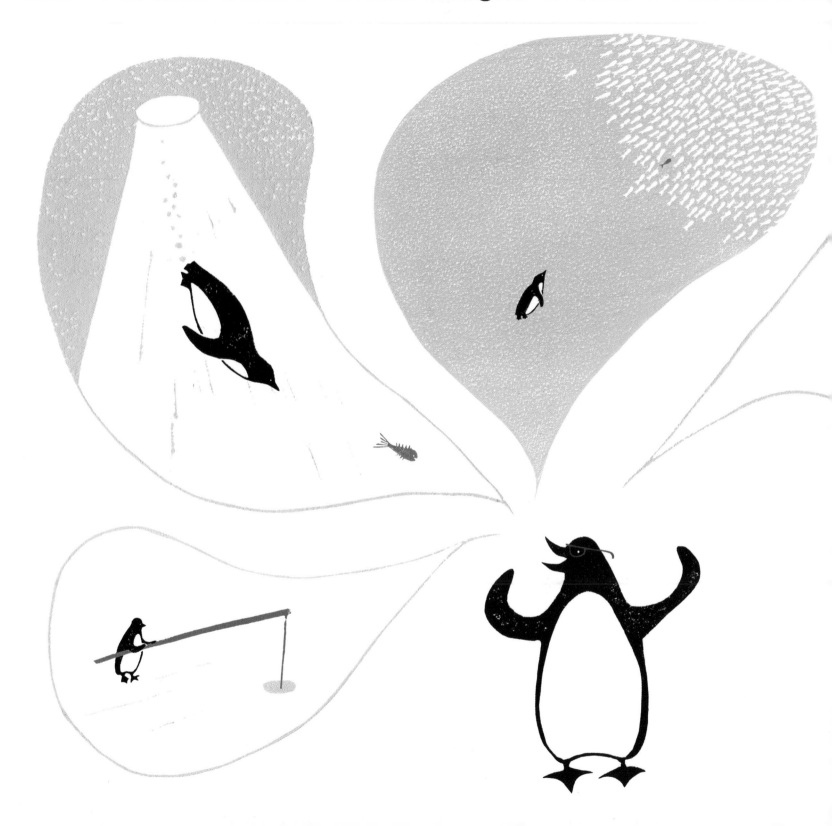

His clothes didn't fit so well,

and he spent a lot of
time in the bathroom.

Perhaps he was just
getting older,

but I kept finding him in
the strangest places.

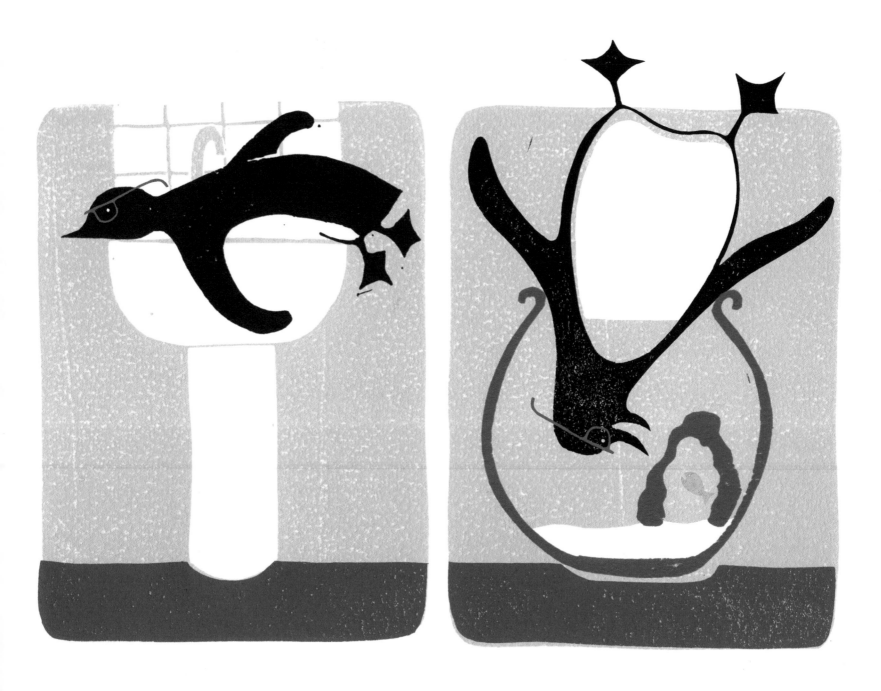

It was all a
bit fishy.

Then one day
the zoo called.

"I think there may have
been a bit of
a mix-up."

So we went to the zoo to sort it out.

The penguin went back to
the penguin enclosure . . .

... and Grandad came home with me.